CAN YOU SOLVE THE MYSTERY?™ READ THE SOLUTIONS IN YOUR MIRROR

HAWKEYE COLLINS & AMY ADAMS in

THE CASE OF THE CLEVER COMPUTER CROOKS

& 8 OTHER MYSTERIES

by M. MASTERS

Meadowbrook Press
18318 Minnetonka Blvd.
Deephaven, MN 55391

This book is dedicated to all the children across the country who helped us develop the *Can You Solve the Mystery?*™ series.

All characters, events, and locales in these stories are purely fictional. Any resemblances to actual persons, events, or locales are entirely coincidental.

First Printing September 1983

Library of Congress Cataloging in Publication Data

Masters, M.
Hawkeye Collins and Amy Adams in The case of the clever computer crooks & 8 other mysteries.

(Can you solve the mystery? ; #5)
Contents: The case of the clever computer crooks — The secret of the emerald brooch — The case of the new wave rip-off — [etc.]
[1. Mystery and detective stories. 2. Literary recreations.] I. Title. II. Title: Hawkeye Collins and Amy Adams in the case of the clever computer crooks & 8 other mysteries. III. Title: Case of the clever computer thieves & 8 other mysteries.
IV. Series: Masters, M. Can you solve the mystery? ; #5.
PZ7.M42392Hawk 1983 [Fic] 83-11435
ISBN 0-915658-11-9 (pbk.)

Printed in the United States of America

ISBN (paperback) 0-915658-11-9

"The Secret of the Emerald Brooch" by Andrew Kantar.
All other stories written by Lani and David Havens.
Illustrations by Stephen Cardot and Brett Gadbois.

Editor: Kathe Grooms
Assistant Editor: Louise Delagran
Consulting Editor: R.D. Zimmerman
Design: Terry Dugan
Production: John Ware, Donna Ahrens, Pamela Barnard
Cover Art: Robert Sauber

CONTENTS

READ THE SOLUTIONS IN YOUR MIRROR

Would you like to become a member of the CYSTM?™ Reading Panel? See details on page 95.

Amy Adams

Hawkeye Collins

Young Sleuths Detect Fun in Mysteries

By Alice Cory
Staff Writer

Lakewood Hills has two new super sleuths watching over its citizens. They are Christopher "Hawkeye" Collins and Amy Amanda Adams, both 12 years old and sixth-grade students at Lakewood Hills Elementary.

Christopher Collins, the popular, blond, blue-eyed sleuth of 128 Crestview Drive, is better known by his nickname, "Hawkeye." His father, Peter Collins, who is an attorney downtown, explains, "We started calling him Hawkeye many years ago because he notices everything, even tiny details. That's what makes him so good at solving mysteries." His mother, Linda Collins, a real estate agent, agrees: "Yes, but he

Sleuths continued on page 4A

Lakewood Hills Herald Thurs., Mar. 17, 1983 4A

Sleuths continued from page 2A

also started to draw at a very early age. His sketches capture everything he sees. He draws clues or the scene of the crime — or anything else that will help solve a mystery."

Amy Adams, a spitfire with red hair and sparkling green eyes, lives right across the street, at 131 Crestview Drive. Known to many as the star of the track team, she is also a star math student. "She's quick of mind, quick of foot and quick of temper," says her teacher, Ted Bronson, chuckling. "And she's never intimidated." Not only do she and Hawkeye share the same birthday, but also the same love of mysteries.

"If something's wrong," says Amy, leaning on her ten-speed, "you just can't look the other way."

"Right," says Hawkeye, pulling his ever-present sketch pad and pencil from his back pocket. "And if we can't solve a case right away, I'll do a drawing of the scene of the crime. When we study my sketch, we can usually figure out what happened."

When the two detectives are not playing video games or soccer (Hawkeye is the captain of the sixth-grade team), they can often be seen biking around town, making sure justice is done. Occasionally aided by Hawkeye's frisky golden retriever, Nosey, and Amy's six-year-old sister, Lucy, they've solved every case they've handled to date.

How did the two get started in the detective business?

It all started last year at Lakewood Hills Elementary's Career Days. There the two met Sergeant Treadwell, one of Lakewood Hills' best-known policemen. Of Hawkeye and Amy, Sergeant Treadwell proudly brags, "They're terrific. Right after we met, one of the teachers had a whole pile of tests stolen. I sure couldn't figure out who had done it, but Hawkeye did one of his sketches and he and Amy had the case solved in five minutes! You can't fool those two."

Sergeant Treadwell adds: "I don't know what Lakewood Hills ever did without Hawkeye and Amy. They've found a dognapped dog, located stolen video games, and cracked many other tough cases. Why, whenever I have a problem I can't solve, I know just where to go — straight to those two super sleuths!"

"They've found a dognapped dog, located stolen video games, and cracked many other tough cases."

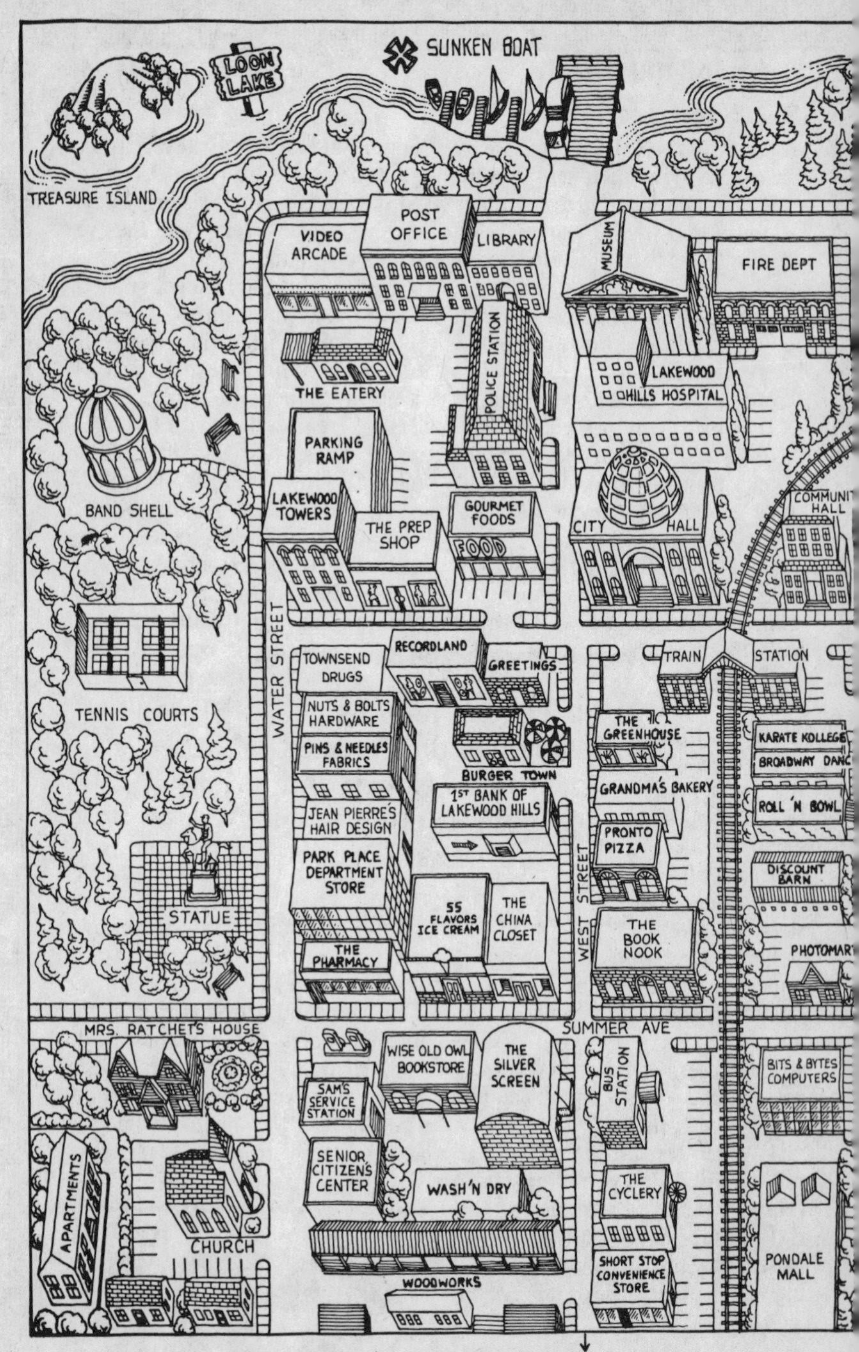
SUNKEN BOAT
LOON LAKE
TREASURE ISLAND
POST OFFICE
VIDEO ARCADE
LIBRARY
MUSEUM
FIRE DEPT
THE EATERY
POLICE STATION
LAKEWOOD HILLS HOSPITAL
PARKING RAMP
BAND SHELL
LAKEWOOD TOWERS
THE PREP SHOP
GOURMET FOODS
FOOD
CITY HALL
COMMUNITY HALL
RECORDLAND
TOWNSEND DRUGS
GREETINGS
TRAIN STATION
WATER STREET
NUTS & BOLTS HARDWARE
TENNIS COURTS
PINS & NEEDLES FABRICS
THE GREENHOUSE
KARATE KOLLEGE
BROADWAY DANC
BURGER TOWN
GRANDMA'S BAKERY
ROLL 'N BOWL
1ST BANK OF LAKEWOOD HILLS
JEAN PIERRE'S HAIR DESIGN
PRONTO PIZZA
PARK PLACE DEPARTMENT STORE
DISCOUNT BARN
WEST STREET
55 FLAVORS ICE CREAM
THE CHINA CLOSET
STATUE
THE BOOK NOOK
PHOTOMAR
THE PHARMACY
MRS. RATCHET'S HOUSE
SUMMER AVE
WISE OLD OWL BOOKSTORE
THE SILVER SCREEN
BUS STATION
BITS & BYTES COMPUTERS
SAM'S SERVICE STATION
SENIOR CITIZEN'S CENTER
WASH'N DRY
THE CYCLERY
APARTMENTS
CHURCH
PONDALE MALL
SHORT STOP CONVENIENCE STORE
WOODWORKS
TO MINNEAPOLIS 17 MILES

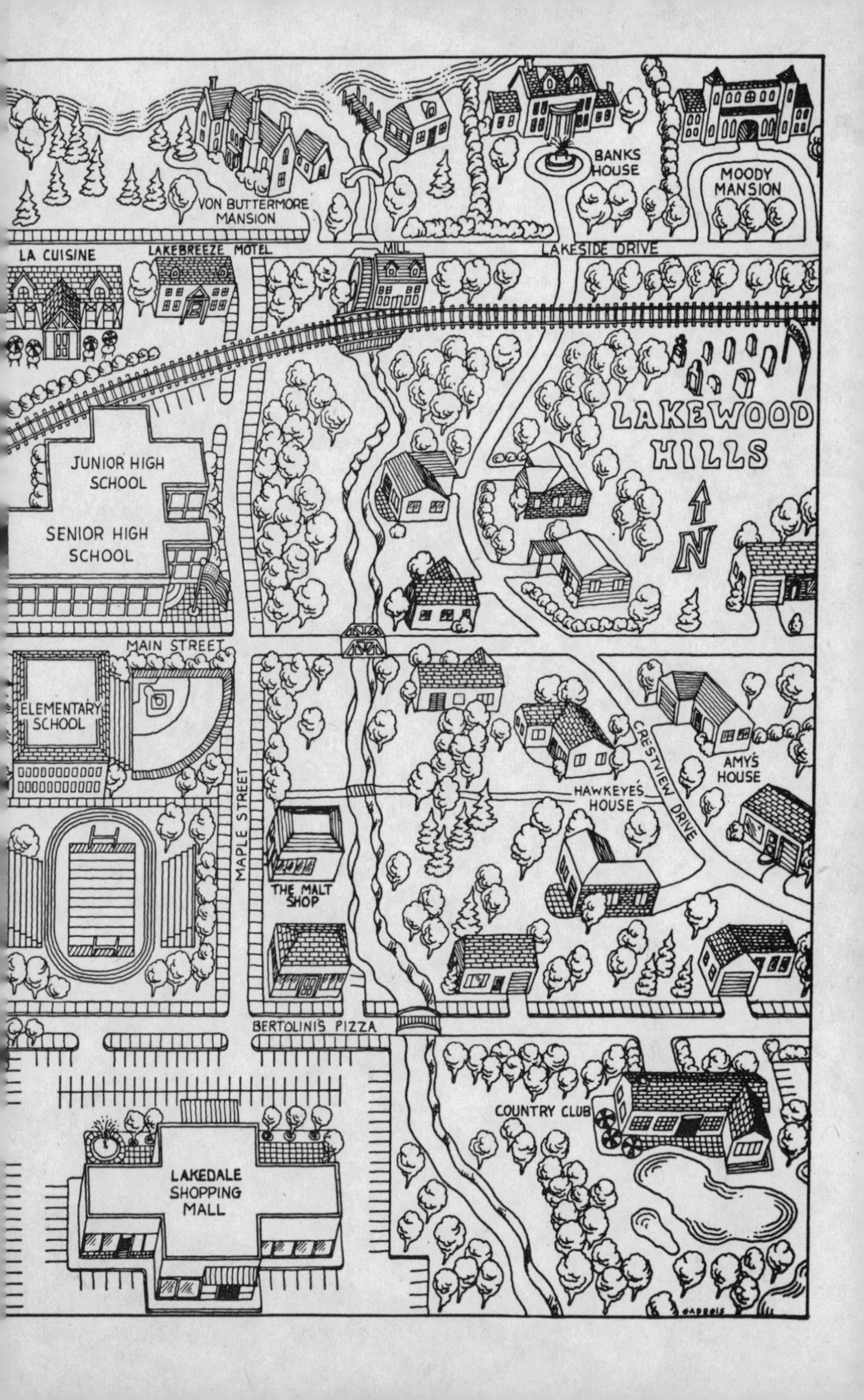
VON BUTTERMORE MANSION
BANKS HOUSE
MOODY MANSION
LA CUISINE
LAKEBREEZE MOTEL
MILL
LAKESIDE DRIVE
LAKEWOOD HILLS
N
JUNIOR HIGH SCHOOL
SENIOR HIGH SCHOOL
MAIN STREET
ELEMENTARY SCHOOL
CRESTVIEW DRIVE
AMY'S HOUSE
HAWKEYE'S HOUSE
MAPLE STREET
THE MALT SHOP
BERTOLINI'S PIZZA
COUNTRY CLUB
LAKEDALE SHOPPING MALL
GADBOIS

Dear Readers,

You can solve these mysteries along with us! Start by reading very carefully -- Watch out for things like what people *say* happened, the ways they behave, and details like the time and the weather.

Then look closely at the sketch or other picture clue with the story. If you remember the facts, the picture clue should help you break the case.

If you want to check your answer-- or if a hard case stumps you -- turn to the solutions at the back of the book. They're written in mirror type. Hold them up to a mirror and they'll look right. If you don't have a mirror, turn the page and hold it up to the light. (You can teach yourself to re backwards, too. We can do it prett well now and it comes in handy som times in our cases.)

Have fun -- we sure did!

Amy

Hawkeye

The Case of the Clever Computer Crooks

After what he'd just heard on the radio, there was no way Hawkeye Collins could go straight to his piano lesson. Instead of biking directly to his teacher's house, he coasted right across Crestview Drive to see his friend, Amy Adams.

Hawkeye and Amy were known all around the suburban town of Lakewood Hills as super-sleuths.

"Amy!" he called, pounding on her screen door. "Bits and Bytes Computers was robbed!"

Amy couldn't believe her ears She threw open the door. "You don't mean Steve's store, do you?"

Hawkeye nodded. "Yeah, it was robbed. I just heard on the radio."

Steve Mikowski was well known in town. Two years ago he had scrounged up enough money to open his store, and he was finally becoming successful. Amy's mother had bought her home computer from him when he first opened his store. Because Steve was a sponsor of the Bytes of Data Computer Club at Lakewood Elementary, a lot of kids knew him.

"Let's go!" said Amy, tossing her red hair as she dashed out the door to her ten-speed in the driveway.

Hawkeye went to his bike and hesitated. "I've got a piano lesson," he groaned.

"So you can't go check out the robbery?" Amy demanded.

"Well, I shouldn't," he replied slowly. "But what if Steve needs help?"

"Right," Amy said, wheeling her bike around and kicking up the kickstand. "I want your super-sharp eyes and your quick sketching hand on this case. Got your sketch pad?"

"Of course—I don't go anywhere without it," Hawkeye said with a grin. He paused. "So let's get going!"

The two sleuths took off. As they rode, Hawkeye filled Amy in on what he'd heard on the radio.

"Actually, it wasn't much," he said. "The reporter kept asking Steve about the robbery, and all Steve could say was, 'How could this have happened?' Then the reporter asked Steve when he had discovered the robbery. And Steve goes, 'How could this have happened?' "

Amy laughed. "Sounds like that reporter didn't get very far."

They reached the store a few minutes later and locked their bikes to the parking meters out front.

"Look," said Amy, "the side door to the warehouse is open. Let's try there first."

They hurried past the store itself to the rear of the warehouse. There they found Steve simply standing in the middle of a large room lined with empty shelves and littered with opened boxes.

"Hawkeye, Amy!" he called out when he saw them. "How could this have happened?"

"What exactly *did* happen, Steve?" asked Hawkeye, glancing about.

Steve opened his arms and turned around and around. "All my computers—a whole warehouse full of them—stolen!" he said, still shocked by the robbery.

"The police just left," he went on. "They say it was a real professional job. Except for the tire tracks near the back doors, the thieves left no evidence. No prints. No clues. And now—no computers! When I closed the place up last night, this place was full!"

Amy gazed all over the room. "Full?"

"Absolutely full," Steve said. "The

shelves were packed. We got the sales contract for the State Department of Education. They're buying computers for all the schools, you know And the whole order was in here—three hundred fifty-six computers, disk drives, videos, and printers. A reporter even stopped by last week to interview me about the store."

Steve pulled a newspaper article out of his pocket. "Here's the article—you can see how full the warehouse was. The reporter had to stand on a ladder to fit it all into the pictures."

"Wow, it was packed," Hawkeye agreed, examining the photograph. "Your business is—or *was*—really growing!"

A little impatiently, Amy asked, "When did it happen?"

"I don't know," responded Steve, shrugging. "And I have no idea how." He pointed up high to a corner of the warehouse. "See that video camera up there? I installed it two months ago."

"You mean, as part of your security system?" asked Hawkeye.

"Right," Steve said. "It takes pictures continuously."

"It must cover the entire warehouse," said Amy. "But who watches the picture?"

"Jeb, my night watchman," said Steve. "He sits in the office up front in the store. There's a monitor there. That way he can stay up near the safe."

"On the night of the robbery," Steve continued, "Jeb was watching the screen, as usual. He claims that one moment the warehouse was full and everything was normal. Next thing he knew, the video screen was showing an empty warehouse. It's as if every last computer vanished in a split second!"

"Maybe the camera broke," suggested Hawkeye.

"Well, Jeb says it's been working fine." Steve shook his head. "And he says he didn't fall asleep, either."

"When did he notice that the warehouse was empty?" asked Amy, checking an empty storage rack for clues.

"Around midnight." Steve put his hand to his forehead and rubbed it. "Then Jeb called the police. And all they found were some tire tracks from a truck, out back. They took some photos, but of course they suspect Jeb is lying."

"What do you think?" Amy asked.

"Jeb has been a good, trustworthy employee," replied Steve. "He's had some money problems lately, but—well, it just doesn't seem like Jeb to steal."

Hawkeye walked to the rear of the warehouse and checked out the loading dock doors.

"Is this how they got in?" he asked.

"Apparently." Steve rubbed his eyes and sighed "The lock was broken and forced open."

Hawkeye leaned against the wall. His sharp blue eyes went over everything, scanning the warehouse. He pulled his sketch pad and pencil out of his jeans pocket. Then, with quick, sure strokes, he began to sketch the area around the loading dock. Often, drawing a sketch helped him to pick out the details that were actually clues to the crime.

From across the room, Amy called, "Do you suspect anyone?"

Steve thought for a moment. "Well, maybe Sam Flannery. He owns the biggest computer store in Minneapolis. He really wanted the contract for the school computers, but we got it instead. I really can't see that he'd risk breaking the law, though."

"Anybody else?" Amy asked, eager to learn all the details.

"The police mentioned that a ring of thieves has been operating in the area. I guess they're after electronic gear, mostly."

Steve shook his head and turned to Hawkeye and Amy. "How could this have happened?"

"I'm not sure yet," replied Hawkeye, still busily recording the scene.

"Yeah, if we can just find some clues or something," said Amy.

While Amy walked through the empty warehouse searching for clues, Hawkeye completed his drawing. He studied it hard, certain

With quick, sure strokes, Hawkeye began to sketch the area around the loading dock.

that there was something there that would tell him how the computers had been stolen

"Of course!" he said, snapping his fingers.

Amy looked up hopefully. "What is it, Hawkeye? Did you figure it out?"

"You bet I did," Hawkeye said. "I know how the computers were stolen—and I think I know who's behind it, too!"

HOW WERE THE COMPUTERS STOLEN AND WHO DID IT?

See page 77

The Secret of the Emerald Brooch

"Isn't this Alien Monster Wipe-Out game the greatest, Amy?" Hawkeye asked as they sat hunched over the game in his living room. The video game was the one that Hawkeye and Amy had been given as a reward for helping to solve a recent computer store robbery.

"Sure is, but don't forget you still have to beat my score," Amy replied, her green eyes flashing.

"Super simp," Hawkeye said, maneuvering the joy stick. "Wow! Did you catch that? I just bleeped two aliens with one space ray." The same skills that made Hawkeye an extraordinary sketch artist also made it possible for him to do amazing things with video games.

Just then the phone rang.

"Oh, rats," said Hawkeye, getting up. He handed Amy the controls. "Okay, chief, you take over for awhile."

He picked up the phone on the third ring. After a short conversation, he came running back into the living room.

"Amy, we've got a case to solve!" He grabbed his red windbreaker from a nearby chair. "That was one of the Madison sisters—Mrs. von Buttermore recommended us to them—and they have a slight problem."

Amy hopped to her feet. "Bad timing. I was just about to defeat the entire galaxy of alien monsters. But who can resist the call of duty?"

They hurried outside and grabbed their ten-speeds. The Madison mansion, which was not too far from Mrs. von Buttermore's estate, was a ten-minute ride away. It was a large, red brick house with a neatly trimmed lawn and an enormous garden full of flowers.

As they climbed off their bikes, the huge, carved wooden door opened and a gentle looking, white-haired lady stepped out.

She said, "Hello, children. I'm Agnes Madison. Won't you come in?"

"Sure. I'm Hawkeye Collins," he said, leaping up the front steps.

"And I'm Amy Adams," she said, right behind him, her red braids bobbing.

Agnes led the way into the dark house, which was filled with oriental rugs and large ferns. As they entered, another white-haired woman was just coming down the wide staircase.

"Sister, who's here?" said the woman coming down the stairs.

"Our young sleuths are here, Sister," said Agnes. "Let me introduce you. Hawkeye and Amy, this is my sister, Miss May Madison."

"Hi, Miss Madison," said Hawkeye and Amy in unison. They glanced at each other and grinned. Hawkeye's blue eyes twinkled.

May came straight over to Amy. "Amy, I must tell you that you have the loveliest red hair. I used to have beautiful red hair like that, didn't I, Agnes?"

"Oh, yes. You were so beautiful. And Mother braided your hair just like Amy's."

Hawkeye scratched his elbow. "Um, I kind of thought you had a problem."

"Oh, of course. Let's get down to business," said Agnes. "This morning May and I were going through Mother's safety deposit box—you see, she passed away."

"Yes, she was a hundred and three, after all," added May.

"Anyway," continued Agnes, "as we were going through her safety deposit box, we came across an exquisite emerald brooch."

Agnes went to a side table and picked up a small black velvet box. She opened it, and displayed its contents to Hawkeye and Amy.

"Wow, that's a beautiful pin!" said Amy.

"Yeah, it's awesome," said Hawkeye. "And it sure has a lot of little emeralds on it. Where'd you get it?"

"Well, now, that's our problem." Agnes forced a smile. "You see, we both agree that it was a gift from our mother. But I'm sure Mother gave it to me for my fourteenth birthday, and May thinks Mother gave it to her."

"Yes, Sister," said May, nodding. "Mother gave me the brooch and she gave you the gold heart-shaped locket with the engraving."

"No, May, the locket was given to me on my seventeenth birthday. I wore it to the prom when Morgan Benedict escorted me," recalled Agnes.

"Morgan Benedict." May's eyes got all dreamy. "Oh, he was so handsome. And Agnes, he truly adored you. No doubt about that." May turned to Hawkeye and Amy. "You know, she was the most popular girl in her class."

Blushing, Agnes said, "I'm sure these children don't want to hear about all that, dear."

"Oh, but it's true," May said.

Trying to get back to the case, Amy said, "Both of you say that this brooch was a fourteenth birthday present from your mother, right?"

The two women nodded and Agnes added, "There are fourteen emeralds—one for each year."

Amy said, "Could I see it one more time?"

Agnes handed the box to Amy. "Of course. Do you think you'll be able to help us?"

Amy turned the box around and looked at it carefully. She smiled and then said, "Hawkeye, would you do a quick sketch of this? I think I can show whose brooch this is."

Hawkeye looked puzzled, but pulled out his sketch pad and did a sketch in less than a minute.

"My, my, Sister," Agnes said as he drew. "Wouldn't that be a wonderful skill to have?"

"Yes, indeed, Agnes," May replied wistfully.

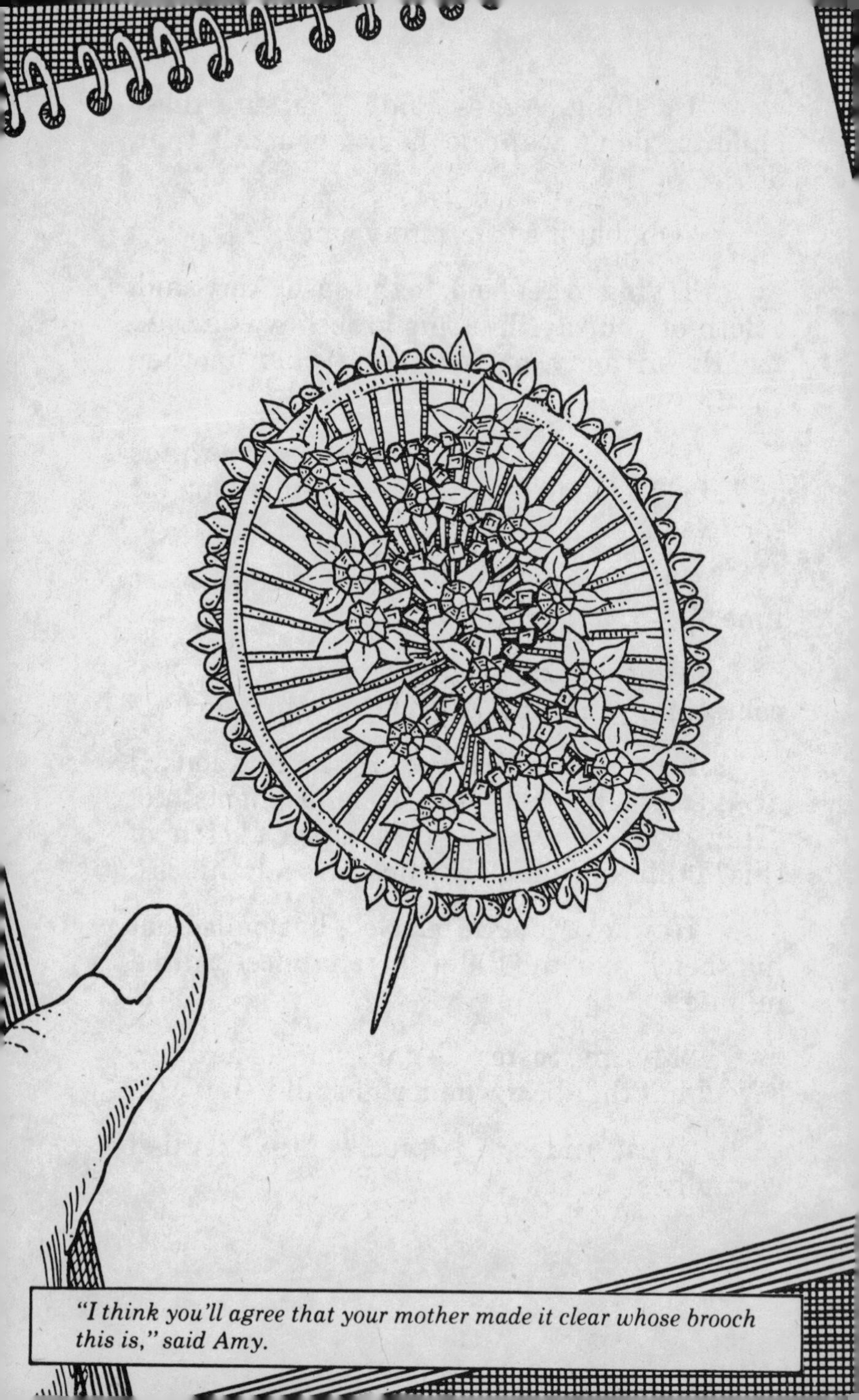

"I think you'll agree that your mother made it clear whose brooch this is," said Amy.

When Hawkeye was done, Amy took the pad from him and turned to the Madison sisters with a grin.

"I think you'll agree that your mother made it clear whose brooch this is," she said, turning the pad around and pointing to Hawkeye's drawing.

WHICH SISTER WAS THE TRUE OWNER OF THE BROOCH?

See page 79

The Case of the New Wave Rip-Off

"What famous general had wooden false teeth?" Amy asked, staring at her history book. She sat on the deck in back of Hawkeye's house, her feet propped up on the railing.

"George Washington, of course." Hawkeye passed her the bag of corn chips. "But Mr. Bronson'll never ask that. I mean—"

From inside the house his father called, "Hawkeye, telephone!"

Hawkeye hurried in, leaving Amy to page idly through her history book. Nosey, Hawkeye's golden retriever, came over to her and barked twice, her eyes fixed on the bag of corn chips.

"Okay, girl, do something excellent," Amy ordered.

Nosey cocked her head at the unfamiliar command, then sat up and begged.

"Good girl! That's excellent enough for three chips!" Amy said, flipping the chips to the begging dog. Nosey snagged each one in mid-air.

A moment later, Hawkeye burst out the back door, his soccer jacket in hand.

"That was Terri down at the record shop," he said. "Her whole shipment of new wave records was stolen. Somebody took every last album!"

Recordland was one of Hawkeye's and Amy's favorite hangouts. They really liked Terri, too. The young store manager didn't mind if kids spent hours looking through all the latest records.

"Let's go!" said Amy, slamming her book shut.

"Nosey, you stay here," Hawkeye said. Nosey watched hopefully, tail wagging, as they left Hawkeye's house.

Heading for their ten-speeds, Hawkeye said, "Terri thinks it must have been someone who had keys, 'cause there was no sign of a break-in. But she can't figure out how they got in without setting off the alarm. Sergeant

Treadwell has already been there. But when he left, he said he wasn't sure he'd come up with anything."

Sergeant Treadwell was one of six police officers in Lakewood Hills. He was a good officer but a poor detective. So he had become a good friend and fan of Hawkeye and Amy. They had helped him solve many cases.

Hawkeye and Amy hopped on their bikes and coasted down the driveway. The two turned onto Crestview Drive and pedaled as fast as they could toward the record shop.

Some ten minutes later, they raced down Main Street, busy with Saturday shoppers, and reached the shop. They locked their bikes to a parking meter and rushed to the store.

"Hey," said Hawkeye, trying the door, "it's locked. The store's closed."

Amy glanced at her watch. "That's weird. It's already noon."

A second later, Terri came to the door and unlocked it.

"Sorry, guys," she said as she let them in. "I was so upset this morning that I just couldn't open up." She locked the door behind them.

"What a bummer," said Hawkeye, already looking around the shop for clues.

"Yeah," said Amy. "So how many records got ripped off?"

"A whole shipment!" Terri pushed her blonde hair behind her ears and pointed to the front of the store.

"I'd just rented all those store window dummies—kind of neat, aren't they? Anyway, I was going to have a big sale of new wave records. You know, I was going to dress the dummies up in new wave fashions and put 'em in the front windows."

"Oh, that sounds cool," said Amy.

Hawkeye walked up to the front and picked up a dummy's spare arm. "Do you have any suspects?"

"Well, some." Terri shrugged. "I'm kind of afraid it might have been Jeff or Bill. You know, the guys who work here. They both have keys, and I know Bill needed the money. Oh, brother, I'd hate to think he'd do such a thing—"

"What about the other guy, Jeff?" asked Amy. "He still works here, doesn't he?"

"Yeah, but he's home sick with the flu." Terri thought for a minute. "I guess he could have made that up, though. For a year, he's been talking off and on about quitting."

"Why would anyone want to quit working here?" said Amy, peering into a box full of miniskirts. "I think it'd be pretty neat. You'd get to listen to all the new groups and stuff, and you could buy records at a discount."

Terri sighed. "Well, Jeff doesn't really get along with a lot of the customers. He doesn't like much of the new wave music."

"That's for sure," commented Hawkeye, turning around. "Last week I asked him about the new album from that Australian group, Men at Work. He told me to try looking in the sewer!"

Terri shook her head, but a smile replaced her worried frown. Amy laughed out loud, and then fell back against one of the dummies. Its head wobbled wildly and then started to fall off.

"Oh, sorry!" she exclaimed, spinning around to catch the head. As she struggled to put it back on the dummy, she tried to get back on the subject. "Um, does anyone else have keys to the store?"

"Only the maintenance man," Terri replied. "He works for all the shops along Main Street, and he was in yesterday washing the windows and changing some of the lights in the ceiling. He put up the balloons for the sale for me, too."

"What about the alarm?" asked Hawkeye, glancing at the bell above the front door. "Are you sure it was set?"

"Yeah, I'm just about positive," Terri sighed. "It's automatic. I have it timed to switch on automatically after eight in the

Hawkeye said, "Terri, I think Amy just figured out why your alarm didn't go off."

evening when I lock up. I shut it off each morning with a special key. And I'm the only person who has a copy of that key."

Hawkeye took his sketch pad out of the pocket of his corduroys. "So no one else could have turned the alarm off and then turned it back on?"

"No, I was the last one here," said Terri. "And the alarm was still on when I got here this morning."

Something occurred to Amy. "What would someone do with a whole shipment of new wave albums, anyway?"

"They'd probably sell them," Terri answered. "There's a good business in 'hot' albums, and someone could make a lot of money even if he sold them for half of what we charge."

"I guess so," said Amy thoughtfully. "Hey, Hawkeye, let's take a look around."

Hawkeye checked out the back door and looked around the storeroom. Meanwhile, Amy knelt down behind the counter to study the alarm system wiring.

Hawkeye pulled out his sketch pad and began to draw the front of the store. Amy and Terri walked over and watched while he completed the sketch.

"Gee, you're good at that, Hawkeye," Terri commented. "It looks exactly like the shop!"

Suddenly Amy's green eyes lit up. "Look at that!" she exclaimed, pointing to the sketch.

Hawkeye glanced up and then back at the sketch. "Terri, I think Amy just figured out why your alarm didn't go off."

Amy nodded, adding, "And it looks like only one of the suspects could have done it."

WHO STOLE ALL THE NEW WAVE RECORDS?

See page 81

The Mystery of the Michelangelo Maneuver

Moments after the phone rang, Amy heard her six-year-old sister, Lucy, yell from the family room, "A-my, tel-e-phone for you! Tel-e-phone! TEL-E-PHONE!"

"All right, already, Lucy!" Amy shouted back from the other room. "It's just the phone, not a natural disaster!"

"Well, then, why don't you an*th*er it!"

Amy rolled her eyes, went to the phone, and picked it up. "Hello?"

"Good afternoon, Amy, dear. This is Mrs. von Buttermore." Mrs. von Buttermore was the richest person in Lakewood Hills. Hawkeye and Amy had helped her solve a number of mysteries and they had all become good friends.

"Oh, hi!" Amy replied.

"It sounds like you have a future opera singer for a younger sister."

"Either that or a baseball umpire with no front teeth," replied Amy. "How are you?"

"I'm fine, thanks. But actually, something quite dreadful has happened, and I need your help. Could you and Hawkeye come over right away? I can send my limo at once."

Amy glanced at her watch. "Sure, Mrs. von Buttermore. But don't send your car. I'll run over and get Hawkeye and we'll bike over. See you soon."

Amy hung up and put on her running shoes, then hurried over to Hawkeye's house. When they rode up to Mrs. von Buttermore's mansion a little later, the silver-haired woman was waiting for them on the stone steps of her house. Her great grandfather, a lumber baron, had built a huge house where Mill Creek led out of Loon Lake, near his lumber mill.

"Now, that's what I call fast!" Mrs. von Buttermore called to them, nervously twisting a thick gold bracelet on her wrist.

"Well, Hawkeye was only practicing piano," said Amy, climbing off her bike

Hawkeye leaned his bike against a tree. "Yeah, and we hurried as fast as we could. What's happened?"

Mrs. von Buttermore clasped her hands together and shook her head. "I'm afraid I've been rather foolish this time, and I really need your help. The police are investigating, of course, but you two have helped me so many times before "

She turned and started to lead the way into the house. "I've been, I guess one would say, conned."

"Conned?" Amy's eyes opened wide. "How? What happened? Tell us everything, from the beginning."

"Well," Mrs. von Buttermore began, as they walked through the marble entryway, "during my trip through Italy last month, I bought a rather valuable sketch. Actually, it is a page from Michelangelo's sketchbook."

Amy's green eyes widened and she glanced at Hawkeye. He whistled quietly and shook his head in disbelief. "I didn't know regular people could own things like that," he said.

"Oh, yes indeed," Mrs. von Buttermore assured him. "Now, do come in—I asked my cook to make something for you. You can have a quick snack while I explain what has happened."

Mrs. von Buttermore led the sleuths

down one long corridor, turned down another hallway, and came to the drawing room. They all sat down in front of the large windows that overlooked the gardens.

"I wanted to have the Michelangelo sketch suitably framed, of course," Mrs. von Buttermore continued. "So yesterday I made the arrangements with the Naples Art Company here in town. It's the most reputable art dealer around and they had the most beautiful rosewood frame."

There was a gentle knock on the door and Henry, the butler, came in carrying a large silver tray with brownies, glasses of milk, a pot of tea, and a cup and saucer.

"Oh, thank you, Henry," said Mrs. von Buttermore. "You may put that right here on the table."

"Yes, Madam."

Hawkeye and Amy munched on the brownies, a specialty of Mrs. von Buttermore's cook, and listened as Mrs. von Buttermore continued her story.

"Anyway, two men came at noon today in a red van with 'Naples Art Company' painted in gold on the side. They handled the sketch very carefully—I was, of course, glad to see that."

Mrs. von Buttermore paused and poured herself a cup of tea.

"But after they left," she continued, "I kept thinking about that rosewood frame. Though it was beautiful, about an hour later I changed my mind about it. A genuine Michelangelo sketch really demands a gold frame, don't you think?" she asked, turning to Amy.

"Um, sure," Amy replied.

Hawkeye shrugged. "Why not?"

Mrs. von Buttermore took a sip of tea and went on. "So I called the Naples Art Company back and told them to change the order. But they said their truck hadn't gone out yet! Furthermore, they said all their vans are blue!"

She put her cup and saucer down. "And now for the worst part. They say that just this morning, they fired the man who would have picked up my sketch. It appears that he may have gotten a friend to help him steal it."

"That's just awful," Amy said.

"Yes, it's horrifying, isn't it?" Mrs. von Buttermore said, wringing her hands. She stood and began pacing back and forth. "What am I going to do? Sergeant Treadwell and his men are out doing what they can, but—"

"Don't worry, Mrs. von Buttermore—we'll try to find it," said Amy.

"When did this happen?" asked Hawkeye. "When did the van leave here?"

"About an hour ago," said Mrs. von Buttermore. "Sergeant Treadwell has already been here and now the police are out looking for the van."

"Did you notice anything unusual about the men or about the van?" asked Amy.

Mrs. von Buttermore sadly shook her head. "Well, no. I'm afraid I'm not much of a sleuth."

Amy jumped up. "Let's go, Hawkeye."

Hawkeye stuffed the last of his brownie into his mouth. "Right. We might still be able to find them."

"Oh, that would be marvelous," said Mrs. von Buttermore as she led the way out. "But you two must promise to be careful. If you notice anything, call Sergeant Treadwell at once and let him take care of it."

Within minutes, Hawkeye and Amy were zooming down Mrs. von Buttermore's steep, winding driveway. They had just passed through the stone gates and onto the street when Hawkeye spotted something up ahead.

"Look, a red van!" he shouted.

Leaning over their handlebars, the two sleuths struggled to keep up with the van. It gained speed, turned left at the first corner and right at the second.

"We're losing it!" yelled Amy.

"That way! It's headed downtown!" shouted Hawkeye.

Panting, Hawkeye and Amy pedaled with all their strength. Still, it was not enough. The van disappeared around a corner.

"I think it went into that alley!" said Amy, pulling ahead.

Speeding full blast down the street, Amy was the first to reach the alley. She swooped around the corner.

"Look out!" cried Hawkeye, jamming on his brakes.

The red van was right there. A man was pulling something out of the back of it. Amy couldn't stop. She slammed on her brakes, but it was too late. Her bike skidded, and Amy slid right toward the man.

"Oh, no!" she cried.

The man, a large crate in his hands, turned. He froze when he saw Amy sliding, out of control, at him. He dropped the box, spilling its contents all over Amy.

And then it was over.

The man stared down at Amy. He reached out with his large hands, ready to grab her. Amy, terrified, looked up at him, then at what he had spilled all over her.

"Oh, ish! Broccoli!"

The man reached down and helped Amy up, then lifted the crate to the side and, finally, picked Amy's bicycle up out of the heap of broccoli.

"Are you all right, Amy?" he asked, concern etched on his face. He was the produce man who delivered all the fresh vegetables to the restaurants in town.

"Yeah, Mr. Bennett," she sighed, picking the stalks of broccoli out of her red hair. "I'm fine, I guess. And I'm sorry."

Hawkeye couldn't say anything. He doubled over with laughter, dropped his bike, and stumbled over to Amy.

Finally, he gasped, "Broc . . . broccoli, your favorite!"

Amy didn't find the situation funny at all. "Yeah, and I'm gonna smell like it all day, too!"

They helped Mr. Bennett clean up the mess, apologized again, and then went on their way. Amy couldn't stop muttering to herself.

"I've got little green broccoli goobers all over me!" she complained.

They biked through Lakewood Hills, street after street, yet they spotted nothing. Finally, after several hours of fruitless searching, Hawkeye noticed something down a narrow, tree-lined road.

"Hey, there's something red down there!" he shouted.

They cut down the road and coasted slowly along. As they came around a curve, they passed a red van with "Mareesh Parts

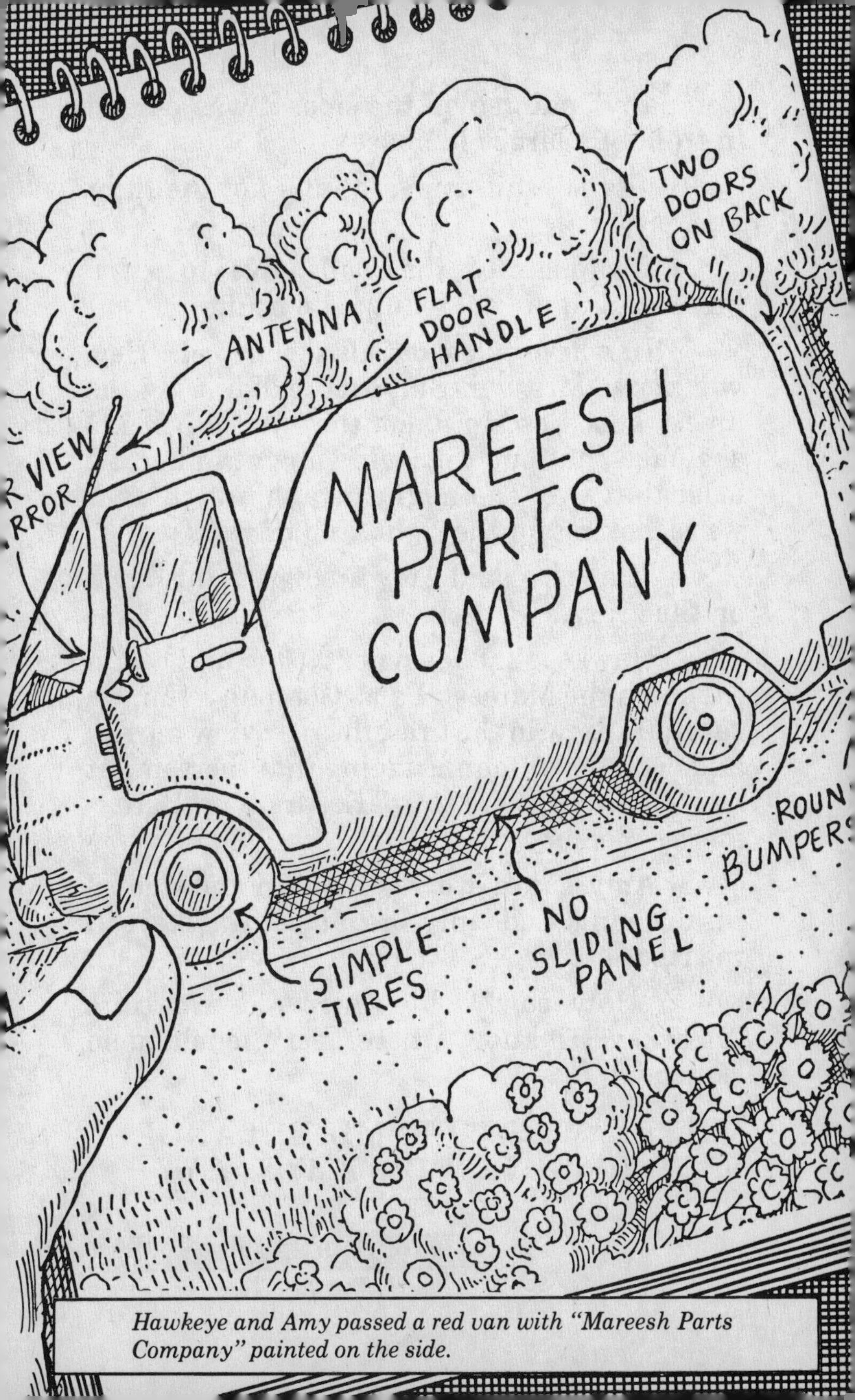

Hawkeye and Amy passed a red van with "Mareesh Parts Company" painted on the side.

Company" painted on the side. It was parked in front of a large old house.

"Rats," said Amy, "that's not the right van, either."

Disappointed, they pulled over to take a break and figure out what to do next.

Hawkeye pulled out his sketch pad. "Hey, you know, Mrs. von Buttermore didn't give us a very good description of the van. Maybe if I sketched that one we could show it to her. At least that way she might be able to tell us if we're looking for the right kind of van."

"Go to it," said Amy tiredly, sitting down on the grass.

Hawkeye sat down next to her and began to sketch the Mareesh Parts Company van. He carefully drew in the tires, the rear view mirror, and even the antenna, hoping that there might be something there to spark Mrs. von Buttermore's memory.

Amy leaned over his shoulder and studied his drawing. Suddenly she jabbed Hawkeye in the ribs.

"Holy cow!" she whispered excitedly. "Hawkeye, I know where the Michelangelo sketch is!"

WHERE WAS THE MICHELANGELO SKETCH AND HOW DID AMY KNOW?

See page 83

The Case of the Rock Candy Caper

It was Old-Fashioned Days and all the stores downtown were giving away free food and prizes. Hawkeye, Amy, and Amy's six-year-old sister, Lucy, made their way down the crowded sidewalk. There were lots of people milling about and eating in the August sunshine.

"There'*th* the hot dog *th*tand!" Lucy shouted. She flashed Hawkeye and Amy a toothless grin and then zoomed ahead. Her blond hair bobbed as she ran.

"When it comes to free munchies," Amy said as they trotted after her, "*her* eyes are almost as big as *your* stomach."

"Har-har," said Hawkeye.

They darted in and out of a crowd of people. As they passed the large glass doors of Pondale, a group of shops built inside an old car sales showroom, Hawkeye spotted their old friend, Sergeant Treadwell. Sarge often called on them for help when he couldn't crack a case.

"Hey, there's Sarge," Hawkeye said. "Looks like there's been trouble in the jewelry store."

"Yeah. Let's see what's up," said Amy. "Wait. You go. I'll tell Lucy where we'll be."

Hawkeye went into Pondale and made his way over to the jewelry shop. It was a small store, but it had lots of glittering gems and gifts on display.

"Hey, Sarge, what's up?" he asked.

Sergeant Treadwell turned around, a worried expression on his face. "Hawkeye, what luck! Boy, I'm glad to see you."

"Why? What happened?"

Sarge leaned on a counter and lowered his voice. "The owner, Mr. Rockworth, called and reported a robbery early this morning."

Hawkeye's blue eyes were already going over the store. "Any sign of a break-in?"

The sergeant glanced over his shoulder to make sure Mr. Rockworth wasn't listening. He lowered his voice even more before continuing.

"No sign at all," replied the sergeant. "No forced lock, no broken window." Sergeant Treadwell shrugged. "It's strange."

"What's missing?" whispered Hawkeye, pushing his glasses up on his nose.

Sergeant Treadwell motioned toward a display case at the rear of the store. "Half of a collection back there. Raw gem rocks or something—stones that haven't been polished. I guess it was part of a special display." He added, "Mr. Rockworth claims that the jewels that were taken were worth more than forty thousand dollars!"

"Wow!" Hawkeye quickly glanced around. "Who had keys to the store?"

"Just Mr. Rockworth himself."

"Sounds sort of suspicious, doesn't it?"

Sergeant Treadwell leaned forward and lowered his voice even more. "Sure does. Mr. Rockworth might have faked the robbery just to collect some big insurance money."

"But you need proof," said Hawkeye.

"Right," said the sergeant, nodding. "Do you think you could scout around and see what you find?"

Just then Amy came in. "Lucy's next door at the chocolate shop, watching them dip chocolates. Boy, is she going to be sick tonight. Hot dogs, ice cream, and now chocolate. Hey, you can even smell it in here," she said, wrinkling her freckled nose. "What's up?"

Hawkeye motioned toward the rear counter display. "A robbery," he said in a voice loud enough for Mr. Rockworth to hear. "Half of Mr. Rockworth's collection of gem rocks was stolen last night."

Sergeant Treadwell winked at Amy and straightened up. Hawkeye lowered his voice and quickly explained what they suspected.

Amy nodded. "Well, we might as well see if the thief left any clues," she said aloud

While Sergeant Treadwell went to Mr. Rockworth to explain who his two helpers were, Amy and Hawkeye looked around the shop. Hawkeye checked out the huge glass door. It had an immense brass lock without a scratch or a nick on it.

"Hey," said Amy, quietly, so as not to attract Mr. Rockworth's attention. "Look what I found."

Hawkeye walked over casually. On the floor behind the counter was a cardboard box with something glistening inside. Seeing that Mr. Rockworth had led Sarge back to the storeroom, Hawkeye slipped behind the counter and crouched down next to the box.

"A broken pop bottle," he muttered, disappointed.

"Shoot," sighed Amy. "There's got to be a clue somewhere. Why don't you sketch the shop and see if you can come up with some thing?"

Something Hawkeye already knew was a key to this case, but he couldn't figure out what it was.

Hawkeye took out his sketch pad and quickly drew the jewelry store, including the goods for sale. Even as he drew, an idea nagged at the back of his mind. Something he already knew was a key to this case, but he couldn't figure out what it was. Suddenly he stopped drawing.

"I've got it!" he said. "I just figured out what happened. And I bet I know where the gem rocks are, too!"

WHO STOLE THE GEM ROCKS AND WHERE WERE THEY?

See page 85

The Secret of the Concert Hall Pirate

"Man, what a crowd!" exclaimed Hawkeye as they passed the front of the Civic Center Auditorium.

Sergeant Treadwell, disguised as a rock fan in a bright plaid suit and purple wig, steered the squad car around the corner and parked behind the auditorium.

"These summer concerts are totally mobbed," said Amy as they got out and made their way toward the hall. She was wearing a green miniskirt and green-and-white striped top for the occasion. "It's hard to imagine the whole place sold out—not even any standing-room tickets left. Somebody must be making a mint!"

"Well, at least it's money that's honestly earned," Sarge said, tugging at his purple wig. "Anyone who tries to pirate a recording of this concert is just a plain rip-off artist."

Sergeant Treadwell had received a tip that an amateur record pirate was going to try to record the Drastics' concert. Then the pirate planned to use the tape to make an illegal record.

"People like that make me sick," said Hawkeye.

"Really," Amy agreed. "They're kind of like, um, parasites. You know—they live off of some other people's work."

"Right," said Sarge. "Well, let's hope we can catch him and teach him a lesson."

Tugging at his tight suit, Sergeant Treadwell led them to a rear door. They were stopped by a big, burly, uniformed guard as they tried to enter.

"Can't go in this way, folks," said the guard.

"But, uh, I'm Sergeant Treadwell of the Lakewood Hills Police Department," Sarge said pleasantly.

The guard shook his head. "And I'm Tinkerbell."

"No, really, I am," answered Sarge.

Searching for his badge, he patted the pockets of his bright suit. "I'm in disguise, you know, and . . . and I know I have my badge here somewhere—"

"Psst, Sarge," said Hawkeye. "Under your lapel. I can see the bulge."

A sheepish grin spread across the sergeant's red face. "Oh, of course. Thanks, Hawkeye—your sharp eyes have saved the day again!"

Sergeant Treadwell turned to the guard and flashed his badge. He cleared his throat and said, "I'm on official business, and the manager of the auditorium asked me to meet him backstage. These youngsters are my assistants."

The guard glanced at the badge and his eyes widened. "Sorry, Sergeant Treadwell. But you gotta admit you don't look much like a cop."

"That's the whole point of a disguise!" replied the sergeant.

The guard swung open the door and led them backstage. Hawkeye and Amy froze when they recognized some of their favorite rock stars lounging around.

"Let's get some autographs later on," whispered Amy to Hawkeye, her green eyes big.

"Okay, here's the deal," Sarge said quietly. "I want you two to post yourselves on the other side of the stage, behind the curtain.

Watch the front rows of the crowd. The pirate—if he's really here—will need to sit up close to get a decent tape of the concert."

As he fished in his pocket, he said, "What do you guys think of my disguise?"

"You look kind of punk," Hawkeye told him.

"No, I feel fine, actually," Sarge replied.

"Not punk like sick, punk like punk rock," Hawkeye laughed.

"Oh, sure—punk rock," Sarge replied, confused.

"Yeah, it's the purple wig," Amy remarked. "Only—didn't you know that this isn't a punk group? It's a rock band."

Sergeant Treadwell thought for a minute. "What's the difference?" He shrugged. "Ah, never mind. Just so I don't look like a cop. Oh, good, here it is."

From his pocket he took out a small metal box with a clip on the side.

"This is a silent beeper," he said, handing it to Amy. "Slip it into your skirt pocket. If you need me, just push this button. It'll make my beeper vibrate. No noise—you get it?"

"We got it," said Hawkeye. "If we need you, we'll just give you a buzz, right?"

Sarge looked puzzled for a second, and then laughed. "Oh, right—I get it. You'll buzz and I'll feel the buzz."

"Maybe a drawing will help. But it's not going to be easy," Hawkeye muttered.

Amy rolled her eyes. "You sure you don't want one of us to stay with you? Well, all right. Come on, Hawkeye."

Hawkeye and Amy crossed the stage. From their position behind the curtain, they could view the whole audience.

"I sure don't see anything that looks like a tape recorder," said Amy, peering out over the audience.

"I don't, either." Hawkeye reached into his back pocket for his sketch pad. "Maybe a drawing will help. But it's not going to be easy," he muttered. "People are moving around so much."

He began to draw as much of the audience as he could. He searched for anyone acting strangely or carrying unusual bags or purses. In a few minutes, the paper was filled with all the details of the scene before him.

"Now it's going to be really tough," said Amy as the auditorium lights dimmed and the fans started to clap and whistle like mad. "Crum. Where is that pirate?"

Hawkeye noticed something in his drawing. "He's—right—here!" he exclaimed, pointing to his sketch. "Amy, give Sarge a buzz—the pirate is right out there!"

WHERE WAS THE PIRATE? HOW WAS HE GOING TO TAPE THE CONCERT?

See page 87

The Case of the Bogus Bigfoot

"Hey, Hawkeye," called Amy from the back hall, where she was taking off her blue moon boots. "Did you get that entry blank out of the newspaper today?"

"Entry blank?" said Hawkeye as he let out a big yawn and scratched his blond hair. "What entry blank?"

"The one for the newspaper's Christmas contest," replied Amy, coming into the kitchen. She gave Nosey, Hawkeye's golden retriever, a big hug.

"The *Lakewood Hills Herald* is giving away ten pairs of cross-country skis, but to enter the drawing you've got to have one of their official entry blanks," she explained. "Lucy beat me to the paper this morning."

"Lucy—up before you?" asked Hawkeye. "On a Saturday?"

"Yeah, I guess, because the entry blank was already ripped out when I got the paper off the front porch." Amy rolled her green eyes. "And then she had the nerve to pretend she was still asleep!"

"Come on, Nosey," said Hawkeye, heading for the front door. "Let's go get the paper. Maybe I could win those skis."

The two of them bounded off just as Hawkeye's mother came into the kitchen.

"Well, hello there, Amy," said Mrs. Collins. She poured herself a cup of coffee. "Would you like some breakfast? I was just going to fix pancakes."

"Yum. Pancakes!" Amy licked her lips. "Sure!"

Nosey, the newspaper in her mouth, came running back into the kitchen with Hawkeye chasing after her. She gave up the paper only after Hawkeye had given her a dog biscuit.

"Nosey, all you do is think about your stomach," said Hawkeye.

Mrs. Collins laughed as she took the batter out of the refrigerator. "Now I know where you get it from, Hawkeye!"

"Mom!" Hawkeye shook his head, and

began flipping through the snow-crusted newspaper. Suddenly he stopped.

"Hey," he said, laying the paper on the table, "somebody ripped the entry blank out of our paper, too."

Amy wrinkled her nose. "Lucy's not *that* fast. She couldn't have gotten to your paper, too."

"That's strange," said Mrs. Collins as she poured the first pancakes onto the griddle. "Who'd do something like that?"

"Probably someone like Macho Thornton," Hawkeye muttered.

"Macho Thornton?" Mrs. Collins frowned. "Who's he?"

"He's a creep," said Amy, tossing her red hair. "He can't stand to lose at anything. You know, like he's the biggest kid in school and he does great in all the sports, but he hates to lose. *And* he's a bully," she added.

The pancakes were ready a couple of minutes later. Hawkeye and Amy sat down with a big stack each.

"Macho Thornton," said Mrs. Collins thoughtfully as she set a bottle of maple syrup on the table. "Isn't he the boy who was caught stealing lumber from the new house down the street?"

Hawkeye, his mouth full of pancakes, replied, "Yeah, he's always in trouble."

Just then the phone rang. Hawkeye

picked up the receiver and listened for a few minutes, then shook his head. He mumbled something and then hung up.

"The plot thickens!" he said as he turned back to Amy and Mrs. Collins. "Mandy's entry blank was ripped out, too. She said the coupons have been ripped out of every paper on the whole block. I told her we'd be right over."

"The whole block!" exclaimed Amy.

"Mandy said that at first all the kids thought that Scott Fedderly did it, since it's his paper route," Hawkeye explained. "But then they found these really gigantic footprints in front of all the houses."

"Giant footprints?" Amy swallowed her last pancake nearly whole, and raced for her ski jacket. "We'd better get over there fast!"

Hawkeye gulped down the rest of his milk and hurried after her. He had one boot on when his mother called out to him.

"Hawkeye!" she said. "Don't forget to load the dishwasher before you go. Those footprints aren't going to disappear that fast."

"Aw, Mom," he grumbled. "Not now. I'll do it as soon as I get back, I promise."

"*Now*," she said firmly. "I have clients coming over to talk about buying a house, and I don't want sticky dishes all over the kitchen."

"Oh, all right," Hawkeye sighed.

One boot on and the other off, he trudged over to the dishwasher. With Amy's help,

Hawkeye loaded the dishwasher in record time. Then he took a couple of quick swipes at the counter with a sponge and headed back to his other boot. In seconds, he was out the door.

"Good luck!" Mrs. Collins called as Hawkeye and Amy ran down the back steps into the snow.

"Thanks for the pancakes!" Amy shouted over her shoulder. "I'm ready for action now!"

Mandy and her friend, Alicia, were standing in the driveway talking to Scott Fedderly, the paper carrier, when Hawkeye and Amy arrived. Scott, kicking at a crusty lump of snow, was telling them what he thought had happened.

"I bet it was Macho Thornton," he was saying. "I knew someone was following me this morning. Every time I'd turn my back to put the paper inside the door, I'd hear something. And twice, I caught a glimpse of a tall guy behind me. It was so dark I couldn't tell for sure, but I bet it was Macho."

"Do you always put every paper inside the door?" asked Hawkeye.

Scott looked up at Hawkeye and nodded. "Sure. That's what gets me good tips," he said, smiling.

"What makes you think it was Macho who did it?" asked Amy.

Scott shrugged. "Well, he's such a big bully and such a poor loser." He pointed up to

"Are these giant prints just like the ones in front of your house?" Hawkeye asked Alicia.

Mandy's front steps. "And those footprints—look at them, they're huge!"

"Hmm. Looks like this is all the evidence we have so far," said Hawkeye. He pulled out his sketch pad and started to draw the scene before them.

"Does anything strike you as strange?" Amy whispered to him, watching over his shoulder as his pencil filled in the details.

"Yeah, something does, but I'm not sure what." Hawkeye turned to Alicia. "Are these giant prints just like the ones in front of your house?" he asked.

"Exactly," she replied.

"Has anyone besides you left your house this morning?" Amy asked Mandy.

"No, just me—those are my tracks there," Mandy replied, pointing to Hawkeye's sketch.

Hawkeye quickly finished his sketch. Suddenly Amy, who had been looking at the drawing, jabbed Hawkeye with her elbow.

"Got it! I know who stole the entry blanks!"

WHO STOLE THE ENTRY BLANKS OUT OF THE NEWSPAPERS?

See page 89

The Mystery of the Money Box Bandit

"Hey, Amy, let's go eat. It's past lunchtime."

Hawkeye and Amy walked out of their classroom in Lakewood Hills Elementary School. Everyone else had gone to the cafeteria to eat, but they had stayed late to talk to their teacher, Mr. Bronson, about Washington, D.C.

Books under their arms, they made their way down the empty hall to their lockers. As they rounded the corner, Amy stopped dead and grabbed Hawkeye's arm. She pulled him back with her behind the corner, and then peered around it.

"Oh, wow. Quiet," she whispered. "Look, there!"

A man was just coming out of the school secretary's office down the hall. He carefully pulled the door shut, without making a sound, and glanced around. Almost as if he were satisfied that he had not been seen, he scurried away and darted out the side door of the school.

Hawkeye and Amy looked at each other.

"What was that guy doing in there?" asked Hawkeye. "That office is always locked during lunch."

"Yeah," said Amy, "and Ms. McCluskey *never* misses lunch." She shrugged. "Then again, neither do I."

A thought struck Hawkeye and his blue eyes opened wide. "What if that guy swiped all the money we've raised for our class trip to Washington?"

Amy stood stock still for a second, then burst into a run. "After him!"

"Right," said Hawkeye, dropping his books as he raced after Amy. "But we'll really be in hot water if we get caught leaving the building during lunch hour."

The two sleuths dashed to the side door. They hesitated a moment, checked to make sure there weren't any teachers around, and then bolted outside. They hadn't gone more than a few feet when they realized that the man had vanished.

"Where'd he go?" asked Hawkeye, looking around the empty school grounds.

"We lost him," said Amy, disappointed. "No, wait—over there!" She pointed to the tall hedge by the parking lot.

Hawkeye bent over. "There's no cover. We'll have to make a run for it. Try to keep down."

Hearts pounding, they crouched and ran across the lawn to the hedge. Kneeling by it, they peered through the branches and saw the strange man getting into a brown car.

Hawkeye elbowed Amy. "The license plate!"

They both looked at it, repeated the letters and numbers to themselves like a chant, and had it memorized by the time the man sped out of the parking lot.

Amy repeated the license plate numbers one more time to herself, then turned and started back toward the school.

"Come on, let's see if anything's missing from the office!" she said, bounding back toward the school.

But they didn't make it back into the building unnoticed. As they ran toward the school, they saw Ms. McCluskey, the school secretary, standing right at the door.

Swinging it open, the attractive grey-haired woman said, "Hey, what are you two doing out there during lunch hour? Better get back in here before I decide to get nasty."

The words exploded out of Amy. "We saw a man run out of your office! We chased him!"

"And he just drove out of the parking lot!" added Hawkeye.

Ms. McCluskey put her hand to her mouth. "Oh, no! The money for your class trip was on my desk!"

The three of them hurried into the building. Ms. McCluskey's office door was unlocked.

Ms. McCluskey gasped. "I know I locked this door. Oh, dear. I'm responsible for that money box. There's over two thousand dollars in it!"

She hurried over to her desk. Hawkeye and Amy were right behind her. Ms. McCluskey opened the money box.

"It's still here!" she said with relief. "Oh, thank goodness. I was really worried for a minute, there."

Amy, puzzled, scratched her head. "Well, I wonder who that guy was. Is any money missing?"

"I don't think so," said the secretary. "Maybe I'd better count it just to make sure."

Hawkeye pulled out his sketch pad. "Before you do, I'm going to start a quick sketch just in case there are any clues here. It won't take long."

Ms. McCluskey looked around while

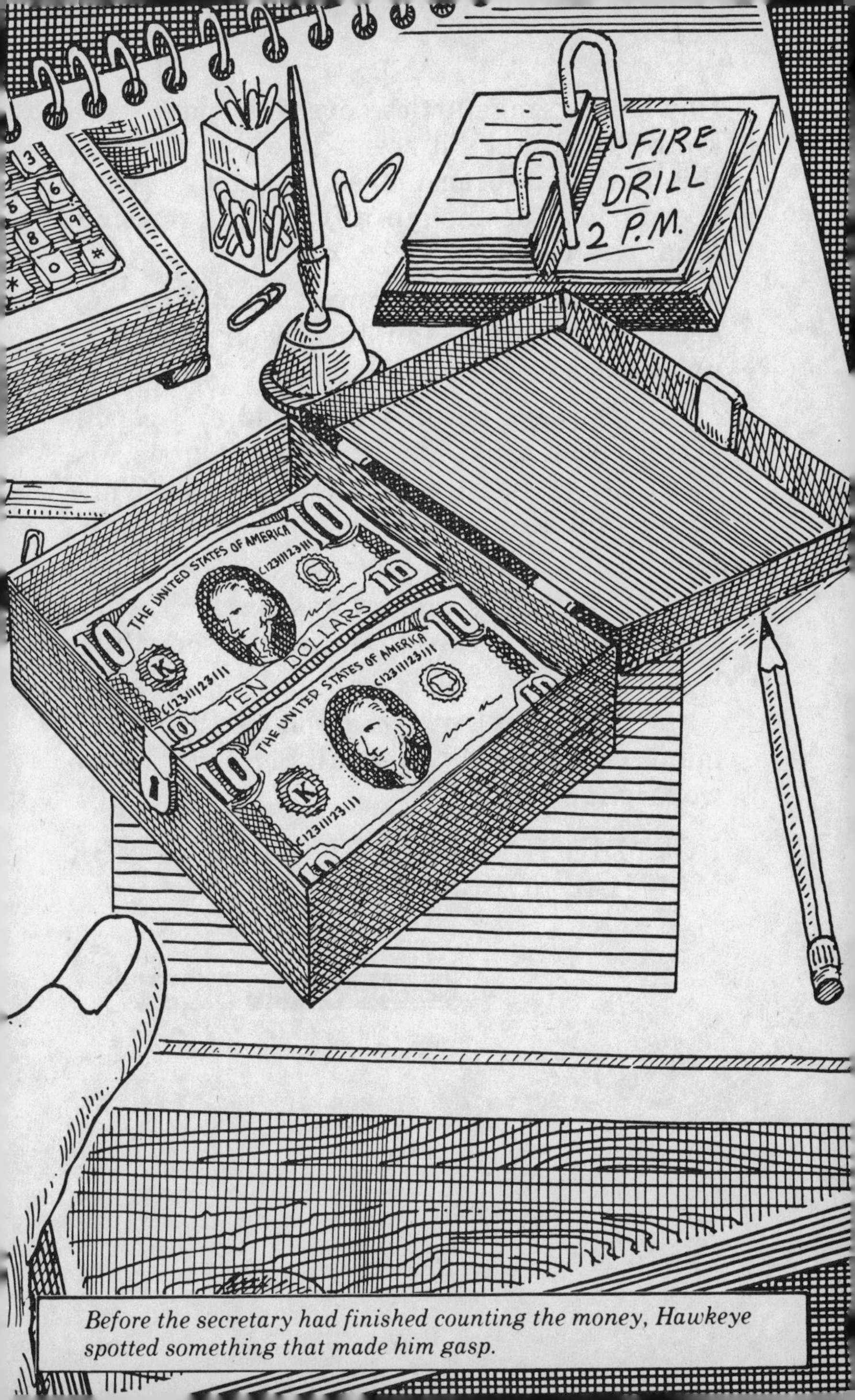

Before the secretary had finished counting the money, Hawkeye spotted something that made him gasp.

Hawkeye's fingers flew over his pad. "You know," she said, "it seems like eveything on this desk has been moved just a bit. But it doesn't look as though anything is missing. What a relief!"

"That's weird," Amy said. "That guy acted so strange—and then your door was unlocked."

Hawkeye put down his pad and pencil. "Okay, you can count the money now, Ms. McCluskey," he said. He nudged Amy. "While she's doing that, let's take a look at my drawing, Amy."

Before the secretary had finished counting the money, Hawkeye spotted something that made him gasp.

"Hey, that guy *did* rob us! This is a major crime! We'd better call Sergeant Treadwell right away!"

HOW DID HAWKEYE KNOW THAT THE MAN HAD ROBBED THEM?

See page 91

THE CASE OF THE VANISHING PRINCE

THE HAUNTED KINGDOM
PART 1

The Haunted Kingdom

Hawkeye and Amy could barely stand still. They were actually in Florida at FunWorld.

"Mrs. von Buttermore, this is incredible," said Amy, her green eyes as big as sand dollars. "I still can't believe you brought us here with you."

"Oh, boy, I can't wait!" said Hawkeye as he looked past them at the glimmering rides of FunWorld.

"Well, honestly," said Mrs. von Buttermore, a breeze blowing through her silvery hair, "I'm so glad you're here. This little trip is the perfect way of thanking you two for recovering Grandpapa's stolen Egyptian treasure. Besides, I had this meeting on Mediterranean gems and antiquities to attend."

Just then a long white limousine pulled up to the hotel.

"Oh, my car's here." Mrs. von Buttermore put on her floppy straw hat. "I wish I could go with you now, but I'm supposed to lecture this morning on one of my expeditions to some ancient ruins in the Mediterranean. And then I'm lunching with the King of Madagala—he's here to show some of his country's fabulous Mediterranean jewels."

"A king! Wow!" exclaimed Hawkeye.

"Well, promise you'll come with us tomorrow," said Amy. "We'll have a blast."

"Oh, I promise. I just love roller coasters." Mrs. von Buttermore started off toward her gleaming limo. "Now, you two have the best of all possible days!"

Hawkeye and Amy looked at one another, laughed, and said in unison, "No prob!"

The entrance to FunWorld was right next to the hotel. Hawkeye and Amy couldn't contain themselves any longer. They burst into a run toward the Magic Gates to Fun World. Towers shot up right past the palm trees, high into the sky. Happy laughter and excited chatter surrounded them, and brightly colored flowers grew everywhere.

Hawkeye stopped and pointed. "Look,

Amy! That's the ride Justin said was the neatest—the Haunted Kingdom!"

Before them rose an enormous mountain riddled with caves. On top of the mountain stood the House of Ghosts, a huge mansion filled with the world's scariest ghosts. To reach the mansion you had to ride a roller coaster car that took you through the Tunnel of Bats and the Cave of the Possessed, and then up through the House of Ghosts.

"Hawkeye," gasped Amy, "let's go! Oh, neat, look! The Looking Glass Maze! Let's go through it right after we do the Haunted Kingdom!"

But just as Amy charged forward, a boy with dark curly hair smashed right into her.

"Oh!" she groaned as they collided.

"I'm very sorry," said the handsome boy, who was about their age. He spoke with a foreign accent, and his large dark eyes looked frightened. "It's just that—that—"

The boy looked behind himself, then back at Hawkeye and Amy. "Could you pretend you know me? Pretend you're my friend?" He glanced behind himself again.

"Are you in some kind of trouble?" asked Hawkeye.

Biting his lip, the boy turned back to Hawkeye and Amy. "Yes, I'm being followed by those two dark men over there."

He motioned toward two huge, mean-looking men who looked as though they had come to FunWorld for something other than fun. One man had a dark moustache. The other was grey-haired and stocky.

"Where are your parents?" asked Amy.

"My mother's at home and my father's at some meeting right now." The boy glanced back at the two men, then turned again to Hawkeye and Amy. "Can I please come with you? My name is Umberto."

"Sure, why not. I'm Hawkeye."

"And I'm Amy. Come on, we were just about to go on the Haunted Kingdom ride."

"Yeah." Hawkeye looked around and spotted a newspaper lying on a bench. He grabbed it and opened it up. "Here, you hide behind this. We'll ditch those two guys on the ride."

Hawkeye held up the newspaper as if he were reading, and Umberto ducked behind it. As they neared the Haunted Kingdom, they broke into a run, dodging in and out of the crowd. They raced past food vendors, and almost knocked over someone dressed up as a huge mouse.

Amy looked behind them. "Uh-oh, those two guys are running after us!"

"Hey, maybe we should go to the police," said Hawkeye.

"No, no," protested Umberto. "No police.

I just want to escape from them."

Umberto took the lead and they reached the Haunted Kingdom just as a train of eight cars was about to leave. The last three cars were empty.

Hawkeye and Amy hurried through the entrance gate and hopped into the first empty car. Umberto clambered into the car just behind them. Seconds later, just as the train was about to leave, two men scrambled into the last car. Amy noticed that they were not the same men who had frightened Umberto.

Hawkeye rolled up the newspaper like a baton and started to tap it on the side of the car. "Get this thing rollin'!" he said impatiently.

The cars lurched forward just as the two mean-looking men reached the loading platform.

"It's very good," said Umberto, smiling for the first time. He fingered a heavy signet ring on a chain around his neck. "We are away from them!"

Hawkeye glanced over his shoulder. "Those guys are really creepy looking."

"That's for sure," said Amy as the train of cars picked up speed and rounded a corner. "Hey, Umberto, are you sure you're not in any—"

But before she could finish the sentence, everything went black and the world seemed to fall out from under her. Screams tore from everyone's throat as the cars plunged downward and downward into the Tunnel of Bats. A flurry of fuzzy bats swarmed arouna them as they reached the end of the tunnel.

"These bats better be fake!" shouted Amy, brushing a bunch of them away from her face.

As they entered the Cave of the Possessed several moments later, they were greeted by a slew of monsters and goblins. Hands and claws reached out and tried to grab them. A whole roomful of coffins burst open and skeletons floated upward. Screams filled the cave.

As they left the cave, Hawkeye poked Amy with the tip of his rolled-up newspaper. "Hey, Amy, why do you think those guys are after Umberto?"

"I don't know," she replied, "but there sure is something fishy going on."

As abruptly as it had plunged downward, the ride now headed straight upward to the House of Ghosts. All of the cars flipped upside down, as the riders shrieked and hung on to their seatbelts.

The cars flipped upright again and headed on through the dark. Suddenly the ride stopped for a few seconds. Dim lights slowly came on. They were in the Chamber of Doors, a long, spooky hallway with closed doors all around.

All at once, ghosts began to emerge from the closed doors and magically float through the air. The army of ghosts descended on the train of cars. Everyone screamed as the ghosts came closer and closer. Yet the ghosts did not collide with the people—they passed right through everyone's bodies.

"Ahhh!" screamed Hawkeye as he saw one ghost come in one side of his body and go out the other. Another was coming right at him. He threw his rolled-up newspaper at it. "How do they do this?" he yelled.

"Ohhh!" Amy slapped her hands over her eyes. "It must be lasers or something!"

Behind them they heard Umberto scream and scream.

Then it was over The ride came to an end and the exhausted passengers greeted the daylight with relief.

As the cars rolled to a stop at the platform, Hawkeye said, "Hey, let's go again!" He turned around. "Umberto, I heard you yelling back there. I—"

His voice trailed off. Umberto was gone.

Amy spun around in her seat. "What happened? Where'd he go?"

Umberto's seat was absolutely empty.

"Look at his seat belt!" exclaimed Hawkeye, reaching behind the seat. "It's been cut! Somebody cut his seat belt!"

Amy gasped. "Uh-oh. What if those two mean guys got him?"

Hawkeye said, "We'd better hurry up. Maybe they kidnapped him or something!"

"Right," agreed Amy. "Let's go back to the place where he screamed. Come on!"

She headed back into the tunnel quickly, with Hawkeye right behind her. A few feet in, they found an emergency flashlight and grabbed it. Suddenly they heard a flurry of voices calling out to them.

"Hey, you kids, get out of there! It's dangerous in there!"

But Hawkeye and Amy, thinking only of Umberto, didn't stop.

"Let's speed it up," said Hawkeye. "Maybe we can still catch up with Umberto and rescue him."

The tracks of the ride led on in front of them. Hawkeye and Amy made their way along the tracks through the darkness.

"Ouch!" cried Amy as she tripped on part of the track.

Hawkeye squinted into the darkness. "We're almost there."

They rounded a bend and came to the Chamber of Doors, where they had last heard Umberto screaming. There was a large camera and light device hanging from the black ceiling.

"When all those things flew out at us, I know I heard Umberto yell," said Amy. "The ride was stopped—so maybe that's when they nabbed him."

"If they nabbed him. We don't even know that for sure," said Hawkeye as he pulled his sketch pad out of his back pocket. "This is the last place where we know that Umberto was still on the ride. Look for clues! I'll do a sketch."

"Right." Amy went over to one wall of doors and ran her hand along it. "Hey, I think these doors are fake. They're just painted on here."

Just then they heard noises and footsteps from inside the tunnel.

"Someone's coming, Hawkeye," whispered Amy. "They must have sent someone in after us."

Hawkeye was drawing furiously. "There's got to be something here that'll tell us what happened to Umberto!"

Amy spotted a crumpled heap of paper. "Look, Hawkeye, here's the newspaper you threw out of the car—and there's blood on it!"

Amy's attention focused on a picture on the front page of the newspaper. "Hey, that's Umberto! He's no ordinary kid. Look at this photo, Hawkeye! It says that the guy with him is his father—the King of Madagala! You know, the king who's here to show the jewels!"

"That means Umberto's the crown prince!" Hawkeye's eyes almost bugged out as he drew. "This is really bad, Amy. I'm almost finished with my sketch. Then we better get the police—and fast!"

The noises were getting louder and louder, coming from every direction and bouncing off the walls of the circular room. Amy peered through the dimness. A man was emerging from the tunnel through which they had come.

"The man with the moustache!" She gasped and was just about to spin around when suddenly she felt a large, heavy hand grab her shoulder from behind. "Hawkeye, I—I—"

She glanced over her shoulder. It was the grey-haired, stocky man, the other man who had been chasing Umberto. He had come through the opposite end of the tunnel.

"I—I—" Amy gestured at Hawkeye, who was still busy with his sketch.

"Just a minute, Amy," said Hawkeye, intent on finishing his drawing. "I got it! Umberto has been kidnapped and I know which way they went!"

Amy gulped. "Yeah, but—but—"

"Just look at my drawing," said Hawkeye, turning around. "Amy, look—"

Hawkeye said, "Umberto has been kidnapped—and I know which way they went!"

Then he froze. The two huge men seemed ready to pounce on them.

WHICH WAY HAD THE KIDNAPPERS TAKEN UMBERTO?

See page 93

CAN YOU SOLVE THE MYSTERY?
TM
READ THE SOLUTIONS IN YOUR MIRROR

SOLUTIONS

The Case of the Clever Computer Crooks

As Hawkeye was sketching the warehouse, he had noticed a photograph on the floor that was like the one in the newspaper article.

"The thieves held the photograph up to the lens of the video camera," said Hawkeye. "That way, Jeb couldn't see what was going on inside the warehouse. Then the thieves cleaned out the warehouse. Jeb didn't notice a thing until the thieves had gone."

Sure enough, when the police tracked down the newspaper reporter who had written the article about Steve's business, he admitted that he had shot the photo that Hawkeye had sketched. Then he led them to the stolen computers. The reporter was part of a gang whose members weren't quite as clever as they had thought they were.

Steve gave Hawkeye and Amy each a new computer game for their help in solving the crime. There was just one sour note to the end of the case—when Hawkeye returned home, he was grounded for skipping his piano lesson.

SOLUTION

READ THE SOLUTIONS IN YOUR MIRROR

The Secret of the Emerald Brooch

When Amy looked at the brooch a second time, she saw that if you turned the box it was in sideways, you could see that the emeralds were set in a pattern that spelled "MAY."

"I think that once I turned the box, I noticed the way the stones spelled out 'May' because they're also the letters of my own name," Amy added.

May clasped her hands together. "And emeralds are the birthstone for the month of May. How could I have forgotten? So the brooch is mine after all. But Agnes, I want you to wear it any time you wish."

"Why, thank you, dear. That is very sweet of you," Agnes said. Then, turning to Hawkeye and Amy, she smiled.

"You've both been so helpful," she continued. "You've solved our problem. We'll always be grateful to you."

"Oh, we just love it when we can figure things out," Amy replied. "Let us know when we can help you again!"

SOLUTION

READ THE SOLUTIONS IN YOUR MIRROR

The Case of the New Wave Rip-Off

Amy noticed that according to the clock high on the wall, the time was 11:10. But she knew that she and Hawkeye had arrived at the store at noon.

"Someone must have set the clock back an hour so the alarm wouldn't go off in time," she explained.

"And that someone was probably the maintenance man," said Hawkeye. "Terri said he was in here yesterday to change the ceiling lights and hang the balloons. He knew Terri had gotten the new wave record shipment. And he's the only person who could've reached up and changed the clock—while he worked on his ladder."

"I bet he came in within the hour after you left last night, and stole the albums," Amy added.

Terri called Sergeant Treadwell, who later questioned the maintenance man. He admitted the theft and returned the albums. As a reward for solving the case, Terri gave Hawkeye and Amy each two of their favorite albums.

The Mystery of the Michelangelo Maneuver

The Michelangelo sketch was inside the Mareesh Parts Company van.

Amy walked over to the van and touched the third leg of the "M" in "Mareesh." The paint was wet. "They just changed the name from 'NAPLES ART COMPANY' to 'MAREESH PARTS COMPANY' by adding a few lines of paint!" said Amy.

She grabbed a pen. "The dotted lines are the strokes they painted," she said as she wrote the name:

MAREESH
PARTS
COMPANY

They rode to the nearest phone booth and called Sergeant Treadwell. When Sergeant Treadwell arrived, he searched the van and found the sketch. He arrested the thieves and returned the sketch to Mrs. von Buttermore.

Mrs. von Buttermore was so delighted that she framed Hawkeye's sketch of the thieves' van, too, and hung them side-by-side in her drawing room.

The Case of the Rock Candy Caper

Hawkeye's drawing showed an air vent on one wall that was large enough for a person to crawl through.

"While I was sketching that," he explained, "I suddenly flashed on the smell of chocolate you noticed in here, Amy. That told me that the vent connects the chocolate shop and the jewelry store."

"Hawkeye, you're right," said Amy. "And that means someone could have entered the jewelry store through the vent—and never even touched a door or a window!"

Sure enough, when they looked closer at the vent, they saw it had been tampered with. Sergeant Treadwell checked out the chocolate shop. Following up a hunch of Amy's, he found the gem rocks at the bottom of a vat of dipping chocolate.

The owner of the chocolate shop was so surprised at being discovered that he immediately confessed to the theft.

After he booked the thief, Sarge took Amy, Hawkeye, and Lucy out for hot fudge sundaes in celebration.

The Secret of the Concert Hall Pirate

The pirate was one of the two boys in the aisles near the front row with casts on their legs.

"As I sketched them, I noticed that one guy wasn't standing the way people do when they have broken legs," explained Hawkeye to Sergeant Treadwell.

"You're right, Hawkeye," said Amy, studying the drawing. "When you have a real broken leg, you put your crutch on the side that needs support—the broken leg side."

Hawkeye nodded. "And one of the guys in a cast had his crutch on his okay side. He's our man."

Sergeant Treadwell and the auditorium guard stopped the boy as he was leaving the concert. Sure enough, his leg cast had compartments for recording equpiment and microphones in it. The boy was arrested and taken to the station to be charged.

The Drastics were so thankful that they gave Hawkeye and Amy each an autographed album and lifetime passes to their concerts.

The Case of the Bogus Bigfoot

Amy noticed that only one set of footprints led up to the house. But Scott had said that he had walked right up to each door to deliver the papers. Amy drew Hawkeye aside to explain her thinking.

"Scott must have stolen the entry blanks. If someone besides Scott had done it, there would have been two sets of footprints leading up to the house," she explained. "Those other footprints are just Mandy's tracks coming out of the house."

"Hey, you're right, Amy," said Hawkeye. "And those footprints are huge, but the distance between them is short. It's like a small person—like Scott—put on big boots, but still couldn't take big steps."

And that's exactly what had happened. Hawkeye and Amy walked back to Scott and explained what they'd figured out. Scott admitted to stealing the entry blanks.

"I just wanted to win something for once," he said, hanging his head.

Scott returned all the entry blanks and apologized to each family. At the drawing two weeks later, Amy's sister Lucy was a winner of a pair of skis.

SOLUTION

READ THE SOLUTIONS IN YOUR MIRROR

The Mystery of the Money Box Bandit

Hawkeye noticed that although there was lots of money in the money box, all the serial numbers on the bills were the same. And he knew that each bill should have a different number.

"Those are counterfeit bills," he told Ms. McCluskey. "That guy took our trip money and replaced it with counterfeit bills, hoping you wouldn't notice."

Hawkeye and Amy called Sergeant Treadwell and gave him the license plate number of the man's car.

Within the hour, Sergeant Treadwell had picked up the man and recovered the money. The class trip was saved.

The Haunted Kingdom

Before Hawkeye could tell Amy which way the kidnappers had taken Umberto, the man spoke.

"Okay, what are you kids doing?"

"Um, we're looking for our lost friend," said Hawkeye.

"Lost?" shouted the stocky man. "You lost Umberto?"

Amy scratched her head. "Wait a minute. Who are you guys, anyway?"

"We're his bodyguards," said the man with the moustache.

"Well, you're too late," said Hawkeye. "Umberto has been kidnapped! But I know which way the kidnappers went."

Hawkeye pointed to his drawing. "They went through the middle door on the right—the only real door. You can tell by the shadow under the doorknob. The other doorknobs are painted on, and they don't have shadows."

"Let's go!" shouted Amy.

Will Hawkeye, Amy, and the bodyguards catch up with the kidnappers and rescue Umberto? Be sure to read the rest of this story in Volumes 6, 7, and 8 of the **Can You Solve the Mystery?™** *series!*

Dear Friend:

Would you like to become a member of the Can You Solve the Mystery?™ Reading Panel. It's easy to do. After you've read this book, find a piece of paper. Then answer the questions you see below on your piece of paper (be sure to number the answers). Please don't write in the book. Mail your answer sheet to:

Meadowbrook Press
Dept. CYSI-L
18318 Minnetonka Blvd.
Deephaven, MN 55391

Thanks a lot for your replies - they really help us!

1. How old are you?
2. What is your first and last name?
3. What is your address?
4. What grade are you in this year?
5. Are you a boy or a girl?
6. Where did you get this book? (Read all answers first. Then choose the one that is your choice and write the letter on your sheet.)

6A. Gift
6B. Bookstore
6C. Other store
6D. School library
6E. Public library
6F. Borrowed from a friend
6G. Other (What?)

7. If you chose the book yourself, why did you choose it? (Be sure you read all of the answers listed first. Then choose the one that you like best and write the letter on your sheet.)

7A. I like to read mysteries.
7B. The cover looked interesting.
7C. The title sounded good.
7D. I like to solve mysteries.
7E. A librarian suggested it.
7F. A teacher suggested it.
7G. A friend liked it.
7H. The picture clues looked interesting.
7I. Hawkeye and Amy looked interesting.
7J. Other (What?)

8. How did you like the book? (Write your letter choice on your piece of paper.)

   8A. Liked a lot   8B. Liked   8C. Not sure
   8D. Disliked   8E. Disliked a lot

9. How did you like the picture clues? (Write your letter choice on your paper.

   9A. Liked a lot   9B. Liked   9C. Not sure
   9D. Disliked   9E. Disliked a lot

10. What story did you like best? Why?

11. What story did you like least? Why?

12. Would you like to read more stories about Hawkeye and Amy?

13. Would you like to read more stories about Hawkeye alone?

14. Would you like to read more stories about Amy alone?

15. Which would you prefer? (Be sure to read all of the answers first. Then choose the one you like best and write the letter on your sheet.)

    15A. One long story with lots of picture clues.
    15B. One long story with only one picture clue at the end.
    15C. One long story with no picture clues at all.
    15D. A CAN YOU SOLVE THE MYSTERY?™ video game.
    15E. A CAN YOU SOLVE THE MYSTERY?™ comic strip.
    15F. A CAN YOU SOLVE THE MYSTERY?™ comic book.

16. Who was your favorite person in the book? Why?

17. How hard were the mysteries to solve? (Write your letter choice on your piece of paper.)

    17A. Too Easy   17B. A little easy   17C. Just right
    17D. A little hard   17E. Too hard

18. How hard was the book to read and understand? (Write your letter choice on your paper.)

    18A. Too easy   18B. A little easy   18C. Too hard
    18D. A little hard   18E. Too hard

19. Have you read any other CAN YOU SOLVE THE MYSTERY?™ books? How many? What were the titles of the books?

20. What other books do you like to read? (You can write in books that aren't mysteries, too.)

21. Would you buy another volume of this mystery series?

22. Do you have any suggestions or comments about the book? What are they?

HAVE YOU SOLVED ALL OF THESE EXCITING CASES?

Volume #1

THE SECRET OF THE LONG-LOST COUSIN

Only $2.75 ppd.
ISBN 0-915658-81-X

A stranger arrives at Hawkeye's house from Alaska, claiming he's a cousin of Hawkeye's mother. But something bothers Hawkeye. So in the middle of the night, he creeps to the living room to study an old family photo. His sharp eyes pick up important clues... plus nine other mysteries!

HOW DOES HAWKEYE DECIDE WHETHER THE STRANGER IS A REAL COUSIN OR A PHONY?

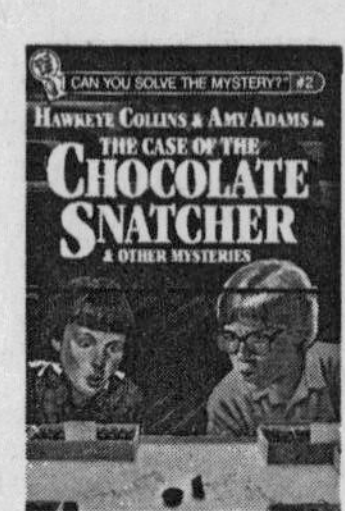

Volume #2

THE CASE OF THE CHOCOLATE SNATCHER

Only $2.75 ppd.
ISBN 0-915658-85-2

A drugstore clerk reports that a masked thief has just stolen a small fortune in fancy chocolates. The getaway car leads Hawkeye, Amy, and Sergeant Treadwell to three suspects. Each of them has a perfect alibi, but Hawkeye makes a lightning-fast sketch and cracks the case... plus eight other mysteries!

HOW DID HAWKEYE KNOW WHICH SUSPECT WAS LYING?

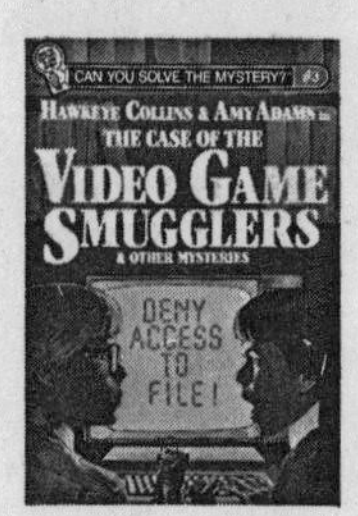

Volume #3

THE CASE OF THE VIDEO GAME SMUGGLERS

Only $2.75 ppd.
ISBN 0-915658-88-7

Hawkeye, Amy and Sergeant Treadwell must catch the crooks who stole the video game their computer club just invented. At the airport scanner gate, Hawkeye sketches suspects who could be smuggling the disk. With seconds to spare, he and Amy pick out the thieves ... plus nine other mysteries!

WHOM DOES HAWKEYE SPOT AS THE SMUGGLER, AND WHERE IS THE COMPUTER DISK HIDDEN?

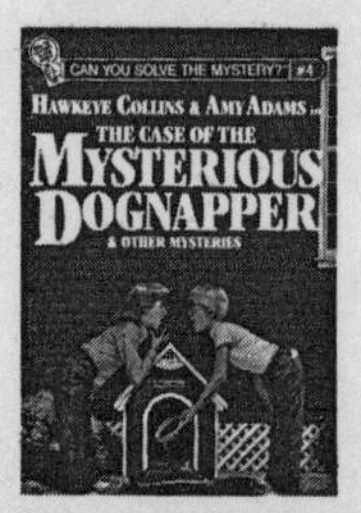

Volume #4

THE CASE OF THE MYSTERIOUS DOGNAPPER

Only $2.75 ppd.
ISBN 0-915658-95-X

While Hawkeye and Amy are visiting Mrs. von Buttermore at her mansion, her Great Dane, Priceless, is stolen. Several people could be the dognapper, but Hawkeye and Amy take one look at the ransom note that arrives and immediately figure out who's guilty... plus nine other mysteries!

HOW DO HAWKEYE AND AMY KNOW WHO TOOK PRICELESS?

Collect all of Hawkeye's and Amy's cases—and solve 'em yourself!